Library of Congress Cataloging-in-Publication Data available upon request

Printed in Singapore
2 4 6 8 10 9 7 5 3 1

You'll Grow Soon, Alex

Andrea Shavick

Illustrations by Russell Ayto

Walker & Company ✹ New York

For three very tall uncles:
Jeremy, Dan, and Piggy
A. S.

For Rebecca, Edward, and Hannah
R. A.

(In conjunction with Bloxham Playgroup Promises Auction 1999)

Alex was a small boy.

He was so small the other children
at school called him "Shorty."
He was so small his big sister's
friends were always patting him
on the head and saying,
"Aaahh, isn't he sweet."

Alex didn't like being small.
It made him very unhappy.
How he wished
he was tall.

I wish
I was tall.

I wish
I was tall.

I wish
I was tall.

He couldn't stop thinking about it. He even dreamed about it.

"Mom, how can I grow taller?" asked Alex.

"Protein," said Mom. "It's about time you had a healthy meal. Then you'll grow soon, Alex."

PROTEIN

So for three whole weeks Alex ate fish and
eggs and chicken and cheese and baked beans.
And he drank eight glasses of milk per day
with Mom's added Protein Mixture in it.

But it didn't work.

He wasn't any taller.

"Dad, how can I grow taller?" asked Alex.

"Exercise," said Dad. "Lots of exercise and stretching. That should do it. Then you'll grow soon, Alex."

So for three whole weeks Alex ran around the garden every day, and skipped and jumped. And Dad made him a special stretching machine and Alex used it every morning before he went to school.

But it didn't work. He wasn't any taller.

"Emma, how can I grow taller?" Alex asked his big sister.

"Sleep," she said. "Lots and lots of sleep. Then you'll grow soon, Alex."

So for three whole weeks whenever it was time for bed, Alex went right away without complaining at all.

But it didn't work. He wasn't any taller.
"Mrs. Green, how can I grow taller?"
Alex asked his teacher.
"Reading," said Mrs. Green.
"Lots of reading and
counting. That should
do it. Then you'll
grow soon, Alex."

So Alex read every book in the school. And he counted. He counted his fingers and toes, and stairs and bears and pears. His Mom and Dad and Mrs. Green were very proud of him. "Isn't he a clever boy," they said.

But it didn't work. He still wasn't any taller. And he was still not happy. Then Alex had an idea. "I know," said Alex. "I'll ask Uncle Danny."

Now Uncle Danny was tall.
Very tall. The tallest person
Alex knew.

"So you want to grow,"
said Uncle Danny.

"Yes," said Alex, "very much."

"Well, first I'd better tell you
what it's like up here," said
Uncle Danny. "Come with me."

"First of all, when you're tall,
you can't fit into a car without being
squashed," said Uncle Danny.
"Oh," said Alex. So that
was why Uncle Danny
couldn't drive in
a straight line.

"And then you have to remember to bend down every time you go through a door," said Uncle Danny.

"Oh," said Alex. So that was why Uncle Danny had a lumpy forehead.

"And then it's not easy to find clothes that fit properly," said Uncle Danny.

"Oh," said Alex. So that was why Uncle Danny wore short pants in the middle of winter.

"Perhaps being as tall as you isn't such a good idea," said Alex. "But I still wish I wasn't so small."

"You're not small. I'll let you in on a secret," said Uncle Danny. "You don't want to grow on the outside. No! You need to grow a bit on the inside."

"What do you mean?" asked Alex.

"Listen closely," said Uncle Danny. And he bent right down and whispered in Alex's ear.

From then on, Alex did all the things Uncle Danny told him to do. Like giving his Mom and Dad and big sister a hug every morning.

And eating a popsicle in the bath with a million bubbles every evening.

And breaking the sound barrier on his bike.

And splashing
the ceiling
whenever he
went swimming.

And telling the
other children at
school one of
Uncle Danny's
jokes every day.

And smiling at himself
a lot in the mirror.
And do you know
what? It worked.
Alex stopped being
the smallest boy, and
turned into . . .

the happiest

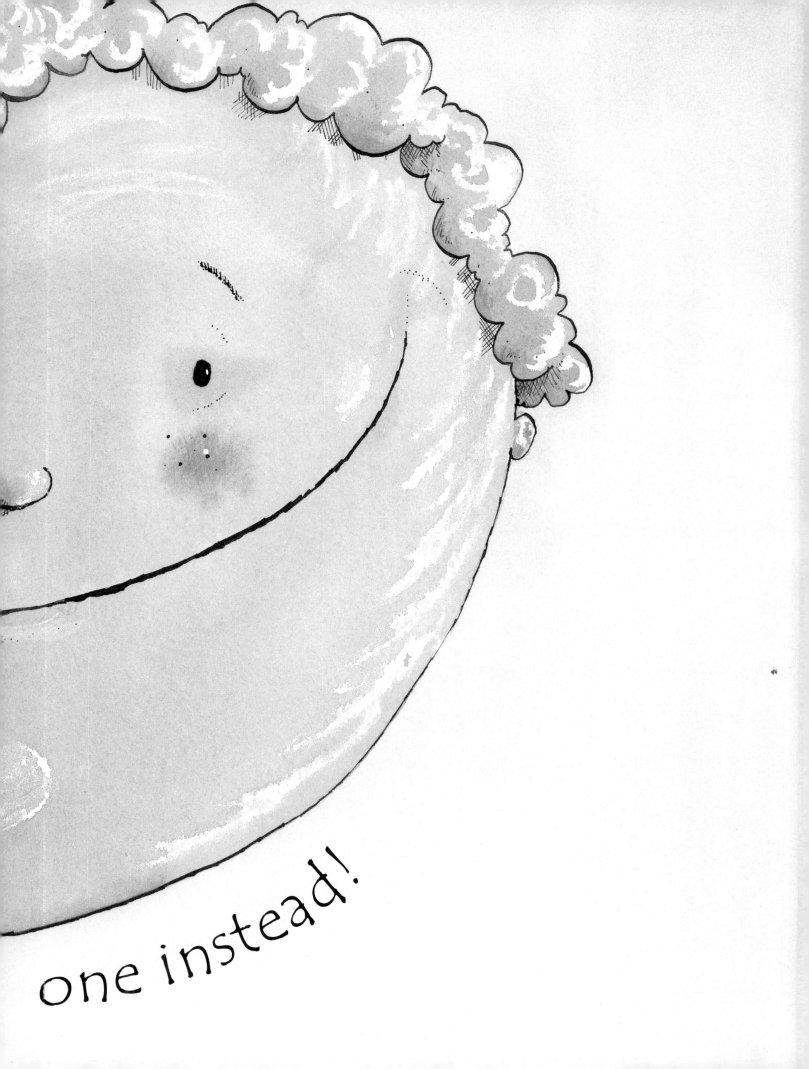

one instead!